First Day in Grapes

by L. King Pérez

illustrated by Robert Casilla

LEE & LOW BOOKS Inc.
New York

Special thanks to Carolyn Folkerth who loved this story from the get-go,
Marybeth Lorbiecki who always believes and never gives up, and
Louise May who has an open gentleness with writers and words.
—L.K.P.

Text copyright © 2002 by L. King Pérez
Illustrations copyright © 2002 by Robert Casilla

LEE & LOW BOOKS Inc., 95 Madison Avenue, New York, NY 10016
www.leeandlow.com

Manufactured in China by South China Printing Co., July 2014

Book design by Edward Miller
Book production by The Kids at Our House

The text is set in Berling
The illustrations are rendered in watercolor, colored pencil, and pastel

(hc) 15 14 13 12 11 10
(pb) 10 9 8 7 6 5 4 3 2 1
First Edition

Library of Congress Cataloging-in-Publication Data
Pérez, L. King.
First day in grapes / by L. King Pérez ; illustrated by Robert Casilla.— 1st ed.
p. cm.
Summary: When Chico starts the third grade after his migrant family moves
to begin harvesting California grapes, he finds that self confidence and
math skills help him cope with the first day of school.
ISBN 978-1-58430-045-8 (hc) ISBN 978-1-62014-190-8 (pb)
[1. Self confidence—Fiction. 2. First day of school—Fiction.
3. Migrant labor—Fiction. 4. Mexican Americans—Fiction.
5. Schools—Fiction. 6. California—Fiction.] I. Casilla, Robert, ill. II. Title.
PZ7.P4256 Fi 2002
[E]—dc21   2001038787

For Luke Toney Pérez. Stand tall, Mijo—L.K.P.

To my wife Carmen Casilla. Thank you for over 20 years of love and support—R.C.

Chico never could decide if California reminded him of a fruit basket or a pizza. His family traveled from one migrant camp to another, picking fruits and vegetables. From oranges to apples they went, from onions to tomatoes to peppers.

They had arrived at a camp in grapes last night.

"Get up, Chico. Pronto," Mamá called as her hands patted the tortillas she was making for the family's meals. "You can't be late your first day. *Ándale*." Let's go.

He'd had so many first days—first days in artichokes, first days in onions, first days in garlic. Now his first day in third grade would be in grapes.

"I don't want to go to school," Chico complained to Mamá when he went into the kitchen to wash. "Kids pick on me. They call me names."

Mamá tippy-toed on a stool like a circus acrobat. She was hanging the yellow curtains that had belonged to *Abuela*, his grandmother. Mamá moved the curtains from camp to camp, trying to make each new place feel like home.

"Listen," Mamá said. "We all have jobs, and school is yours."

Mamá jumped down from the stool and put one hand on Chico's shoulder, the other on his back. She straightened him up until he looked like Papá before he went to work in the fields each day. Chico wondered why Mamá kept doing that. Sure as grapes turn purple, she stood him tall when he went to school.

Mamá didn't know how scary school could be. She didn't understand that some kids didn't like him. Maybe it was because he often moved before kids got to know him, or because he spoke Spanish sometimes. Besides, Chico figured he didn't need to go to school that much. He wanted to be a race car driver, driving fast, winning a big trophy. *Va-ROOM!* They didn't teach you how to drive race cars in school.

At the bus stop Chico *va-room*ed over to a few kids he had seen in other camps.

"*Hola,*" he said, steering around them. Hello.

"*Hola,*" they shouted back.

When the bus came, the driver looked mean as a crew boss.

"Hurry up!" the bus driver boomed before Chico or the others could find places to sit. "Move it!"

The bus lurched forward. Chico grabbed the back of a seat and held on.

"You better watch out or Old Hoonch will get you," the boy sitting there warned Chico.

So that's Old Hoonch from grapes, Chico thought, staring at the driver. He was so mean, kids in other camps talked about him. They joked it'd take a pot of tamales to fill up Old Hoonch and make him nice.

Two boys in the first row bounced on their seats and shoved each other.

"Hey, new kid," one of the boys called to Chico. "What are you looking at?" They didn't seem afraid of Old Hoonch, even though he frowned at them in the mirror.

"You better watch out for those troublemakers too," Chico's seatmate said. "Mike and Tony—they're mean kids in fourth grade."

At school the office secretary told Chico to go to room 8. There, George Washington's picture hung above the chalkboard. Chico silently greeted his old friend from other schools. *Buenos días, amigo.*

The teacher's name was Ms. Andrews. "Welcome, Chico," she said. "You can sit there, by John Evans."

John looked friendlier than many of the kids he'd met in other schools.

"You're lucky you're in this class," John said. "Ms. Andrews is the best teacher. She can crack a home run over the playground fence, and every time she rounds home, she gives a loud cheer."

Chico's eyes got big as lemons.

"You fooling me?" Chico said. He wondered how a little *senorita* like Ms. Andrews could hit a ball so far. She cheers for herself?

During the pledge of allegiance, Chico felt goose bumps on his arms. The pledge made him feel proud to be an American, even though some people treated him like a foreigner.

Ms. Andrews asked the two new students to tell the class about themselves.

Sylvie, a girl from camp, stood and took a little bow.

"My name is Sylvie Castro," she said. "I have two brothers and two sisters, but I'd rather have a kitten." Everyone laughed, even Ms. Andrews.

Now Chico saw the whole class looking his way. George Washington too. Chico had to say something.

"I'm Chico Padilla. My papá picks more crates than his friends Juan Grande and Juan Chiquito together. He's real quick."

Then Chico was quick too. He sat down, fast. The class was quiet, but Ms. Andrews smiled at him.

Ms. Andrews likes me, Chico thought. He would try to work hard for her. He wondered if he should have told about himself, about how he could dance the bull dance while his uncles played *salsa* on guitars, or how he wanted to be a race car driver.

Next Ms. Andrews put out some pictures. "Choose a picture you like," she told the class, "and write a story about it."

Chico picked a white house with bushes and flowers. He bet that house had a room for cooking, another room for bathing, and bedrooms for everybody. It probably even had hot water and a TV!

Chico didn't like writing. It was hard to find the right words, but he did his best for Ms. Andrews.

My house she is OK, Chico struggled to write. *The paint is coming off. A little hole in the floor. Someday I'll have a nice house like this.*

During math, Ms. Andrews called on Chico.

"Fourteen plus forty-five is . . . ?" Ms. Andrews asked.

Chico picked up the chalk and wrote 59. It was easy as adding the crates of fruits and vegetables Papá picked.

Ms. Andrews winked. "Let's try fifty-eight plus thirty-six." In a flash Chico wrote 94.

Ms. Andrews' eyebrows shot up. "Can you do fifty-nine plus ninety-four?"

Chico thought for a second. Then he wrote 153.

"Oh, YES!" said Ms. Andrews, giving a thumbs-up.

Chico hadn't felt this good since he'd broken the piñata at the harvest picnic.

"I bet you'd like the Math Fair," John told Chico when he got back to his desk. "It's next month."

Chico knew about math fairs. They had one at the school in radishes and the school in dates, but his family always moved before he could compete. Quickly Chico added up the weeks they'd be in grapes. If they stayed through raisins, maybe he'd get to go to the Math Fair.

This first day isn't so bad, Chico thought, sitting at a lunch table. He peeled a grape and popped it into his mouth. It felt smooth and cool. Nothing scary had happened, and there would be the Math Fair.

Just then Mike and Tony, the troublemakers from the bus, came over to Chico's table.

"Oh, yum, yum. Let's see what this new kid eats," Mike said, grabbing Chico's lunch sack.

"Looky here," said Tony, holding up a tortilla. "This looks like cardboard. Bet it tastes like it too."

Chico's heart thumped. Why, anyone who would say something like that about a tortilla could hurt him bad.

"Betcha his mommy makes them," Mike teased.

"Don't talk about my mamá," Chico warned in a low voice.

"What'd you say?" Mike said.

That's when Chico felt Mamá's hands. Finally he got it! Mamá meant for him to have courage, be strong. Although his knees felt weak, Chico stood up tall.

It got quiet enough to hear cucumbers grow.

Tony leaned so close, Chico could feel his breath. Then Tony pointed his finger and smirked. "Well, look who's trying to be macho."

Chico didn't feel macho, and he didn't feel brave either. He wished he were back at the chalkboard, working math problems.

Suddenly Chico said, "Do *you* know what fifty-nine and ninety-four is?"

"WHAT?!" Mike and Tony said together. They looked surprised.

"One hundred fifty-three," Chico replied.

"Hey, kid," Mike said. "You learn to add counting the holes in your roof?"

Tony and Mike high-fived and bent over laughing.

"Need an easier one? Twenty-five and seventy-two," Chico heard himself say. "Ninety-seven!" he answered before they got a chance.

A crowd of kids began to surround them.

"What if you take sixty-five crates of dried grapes and add seventy-seven crates to it? How many crates of raisins do you get?" Chico continued.

The crowd was growing. Watching. Waiting.

"Leave him alone," a girl called out.

"He didn't do anything to you," someone else added.

Tony looked around. "This is dumb," he said. "Who cares about adding up crates."

"Yeah. Who cares," repeated Mike.

No one moved. No one said a word. Finally Mike and Tony turned, trying to look tough. The crowd parted, letting them walk through.

John rushed over to Chico. "Those kids scare everybody," said John. "But you didn't look scared."

"They scared me some," Chico admitted, but he thought, *Bravo!* He'd stood up for himself, and it felt good.

"You think you'll be here for the Math Fair?" John asked. "We could be partners."

Chico smiled. "Maybe. I'd like that."

That afternoon, getting off the bus, Chico walked past
Old Hoonch.

"Buenas tardes y gracias," Chico said.

Old Hoonch glared at him. "What'd you say?"

"I said, 'Good afternoon and thank you.' You know, for the
ride." He took a deep breath. "And my name is Chico. Chico
Padilla. I live here now, in grapes."

Old Hoonch rested his elbow on the steering wheel and
looked down Chico's lane. "Well, good afternoon to you,
Chico Padilla," he mumbled. "See you tomorrow."

Chico jumped off the bus. This had been a pretty good first day. He had a new friend and a good teacher, and Old Hoonch knew his name.

Chico watched until the bus disappeared in a cloud of dust. Then he ran down the lane toward home, where yellow curtains blew in the windows.